To Opa, Dharmesh and Muddi
for always believing in me!

First published in 2015 by Child's Play (International) Ltd
Ashworth Road, Bridgemead, Swindon SN5 7YD, UK

Published in USA by Child's Play Inc
250 Minot Avenue, Auburn, Maine 04210

Distributed in Australia by Child's Play Australia Pty Ltd
Unit 10/20 Narabang Way, Belrose, Sydney, NSW 2085

ISBN 978-1-84643-911-7
L121018CPL12189117

Printed in Heshan, China

5 7 9 10 8 6 4

A catalogue record of this book
is available from the British Library

www.childs-play.com

Ice in the Jungle

Ariane Hofmann-Maniyar

When Ice came home
from playing with her friends,
her mother was already
waiting for her.

'Great news, my dear,' she said. 'I have a new job in an exciting land, far away. We will be moving in a few weeks.'

Ice did not think it was great news.

She hated saying
goodbye to her friends.

The journey took a very long time.

Finally, they arrived
at their new home.
It was so hot!

Ice unpacked her suitcase and decorated her room.

Tomorrow she would have to go to her new school.

When she met her classmates, everyone stared at her.

During lunch break, the children
asked Ice many questions...

...but she did not understand a word they said!

Soon, Ice was lost!
She felt all alone.
She missed her
old home and friends.

While she was feeling sad, her toy suddenly appeared.

And then she was given a present!

She had never seen such a strange thing before.

Ice copied the others.

YUCK!
It was the strangest
fish she had ever tasted!

Ice did not like her new home very much.
Everything was so different.

Only her mother's hug felt the same as always.
'It will get better, you'll see,' said her mother.
'You'll make some new friends soon.'

The next day,
Ice tried to
make friends.

But everyone seemed too busy doing other things.

The party was so much fun,
Ice didn't want it to end.

'Please can my new friends
come home to play tomorrow?'